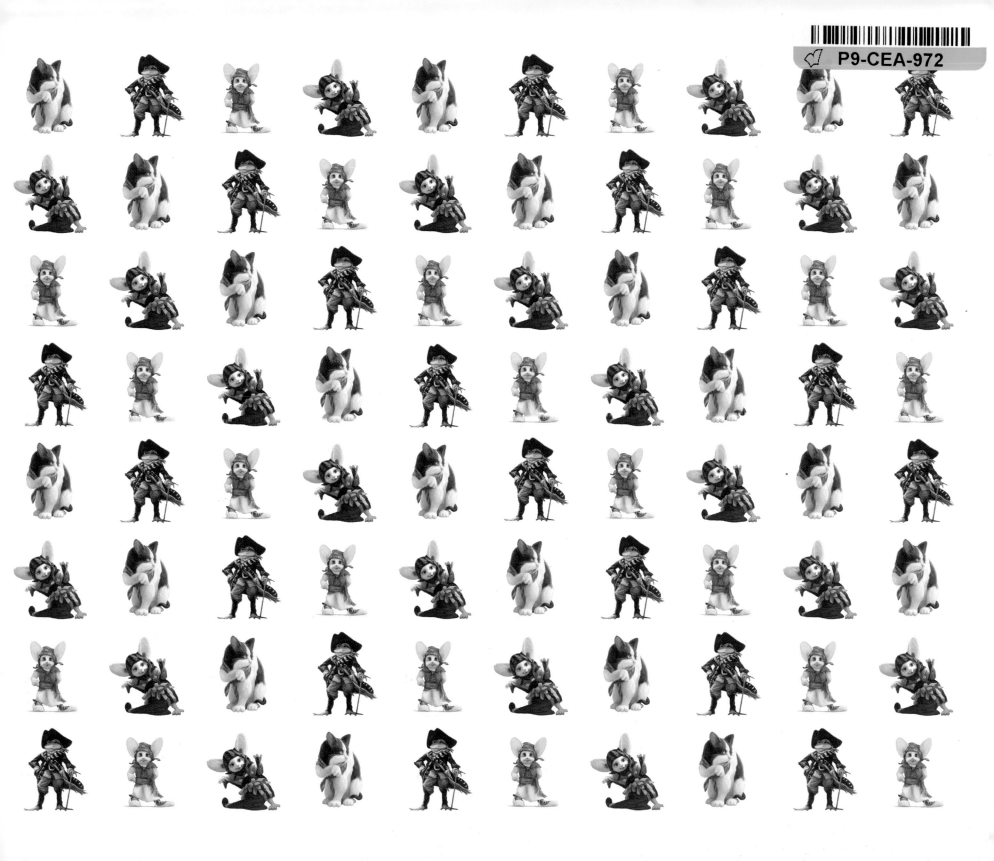

Rip Squeak and His Friends Discover The Treasure

Published by
Rip Squeak Press
an imprint of Rip Squeak, Inc.
23 South Tassajara Drive
San Luis Obispo, California 93405 USA

RIP SQUEAK™ is a trademark of Leonard Filgate

Library of Congress Control Number: 2002092579

ISBN 0-9672422-2-3

First Special Edition - Second Printing
Printed in Italy
10 9 8 7 6 5 4 3 2

Book layout and design by Susan Yost-Filgate
Printed by Societá Editoriale Grafiche AZ, Verona

Very special thanks to Lois Sarkisian, Larry Sloan, and Leonard Stern.

You can find the art of Leonard Filgate at:
www.RipSqueak.com

Rip Squeak

and His Friends Discover

The Treasure

Illustrated by Leonard Filgate
Written by Susan Yost-Filgate

To the memory of Harry, Jane, and Larry–
for teaching us that anything is possible.

Rip Squeak Press

San Luis Obispo, California, USA

Rip Squeak stared out the toy room window. He was thinking that the best thing that ever happened was when the humans went away and he and his sister, Jesse, met Abbey the cat and Euripides the frog and discovered "The Toy Room."

That's when Rip caught sight of an odd-looking figure bouncing up the path toward the cottage.

"I think Euripides is coming," Rip called out. Hoping that Jesse and Abbey could hear, he added, "Looks like it's a day for another great adventure!"

Rip heard the now familiar "THUMP" as Euripides came through the cat door.

Moments later Euripides appeared in the toy room accompanied by Jesse, her doll, Bunny, and Abbey. Even though it wasn't polite to stare, Rip couldn't help but gawk at the costumed frog.

"Arghhhh! What ye starin' at, matey?" snapped Euripides.

"Ye never seen a pirate 'afore?" Everyone giggled at the strange gravelly voice.

"Ye landlubbers, gather 'round," he said, hopping onto the bed, dragging a big book behind him.

The friends snuggled up together as Euripides opened "Pirate Tales." The magic began as he told stories about life on the high seas, faraway places, pirates with peg legs and eye patches, shipwrecks and buried treasure.

As Euripides came to the end, a crumpled piece of paper fell out of the book.

"Treasure map?" Euripides wondered out loud.

"Treasure!?" the others shouted excitedly.

"Unfold it! Unfold it!" said Jesse, bouncing up and down.

"It's a map all right!" Rip announced. "And it sure looks familiar— is that our pond?"

Abbey looked closely at the map. "I think you're right, Rip." Then she asked, pointing, "What do think that letter 'X' means?"

"'X' marks the spot, huh Rip?" asked Jesse, pulling at her brother's shirt.

"I think we have an honest-to-goodness treasure map," Rip concluded.

"Arghhh," growled Euripides. "An' mebbe it'll lead to some pirate's bounty that we can all share."

"Oh, wow," Jesse exclaimed, her eyes glowing. "We found an adventure!"

"First, ye landlubbers, we must dress for the adventure," Euripides insisted as he led them to an old trunk where they found colorful scarves for their heads, just like the pirates in the book. They also found pants and shirts and vests. Soon they were ready to go.

"Wait," said Jesse, as she pulled something white and red from the trunk.

"What's that?" Rip asked.

"Oh, just something we may need later," Jesse replied mysteriously, as she quickly stuffed the piece of cloth inside a pocket.

They headed out the door to follow
the path on the map. It led to a thicket
by the pond. Rip looked into the
darkness and felt his stomach quiver.
"It's pretty scary in there," he said in
a shaky voice.

"Looks buggy to me," said Abbey,
scrunching up her nose.

"Bugs aren't so bad, Abbey,"
Euripides replied.

"Easy for you to say– you're
a frog," Abbey teased, licking
her clean, thick fur.

"This is the way. Come on," urged Rip,
trying to be brave and forget his own fears.

Euripides pulled out his walking stick and held
it up like a pirate's cutlass. "Let's go, me hearties!"

Abbey took a last lick at her fur. "One for all
and all for one," she said, trying to sound enthused.

Euripides led the way, clearing the path. Rip carried the map.
Euripides called him "The Navigator," which Rip really liked. It was a
hard job, looking for landmarks and following the map through the dense thicket.

As they walked along, Euripides began to sing a song about bugs and creepy crawly things. Soon they were all singing it, even Abbey. Singing always made them feel better.

"In the thicket, icky-wicky crawly things peer out at us.
But we're to-gether, so we don't fuss
'Cause it's such a pleasure (Ooh, what was that?)
Searching for— unknown treasure."

As the friends moved through the thicket, Rip tripped over the roots of a tree and the map flew out of his hand. "The map, the map!" he yelled. "Where's the map?"

Everyone began to search.

"There it is!" said Abbey, who was quite good at seeing in the dark.

"Where?" Rip asked.

"There," Abbey pointed— and sure enough, there it was, in a berry bush.

Rip reached in as far as he could— "I can't quite—"

"Come on, Rip, we'll never find the treasure without it," Jesse said anxiously.

"Uhhh. . ." grunted Rip, making one final stretch. "Got it!"

When Rip pulled out the map and shook it off, a big black
ant yelled, "Hey, watch it, you!" as he tumbled to the ground.

"Yeah, that hurt!" said the other ant, shaking himself off and
standing up.

"Sorry," Rip said, startled. "We didn't want you eating our map."

"A map? Like a treasure map?" the tall ant questioned.

"Yep," Jesse responded proudly.

The tall ant's eyes lit up. "Does it lead to a food-kinda-treasure?"
he asked.

"Yeah, like a cookie-kinda-treasure?" added the short one.

"Well, gentlemen, You're in luck," Euripides said, pulling two big
cookies from his pocket.

"Wow!" the ants exclaimed in unison.

"We don't mean to be ungrateful," said the tall ant, taking a
bite out of his cookie, "but, gotta go now."

"Yeah, hate to eat and run," said the shorter ant as
he shuffled off with his *treasure*.

When the ants
disappeared
from sight,
Jesse urged
everyone on.

"Let's go see
what *our* treasure
is."

As the adventurers continued, they suddenly heard something coming right toward them!

"Duck!" yelled Abbey. Rip, Jesse, and Euripides fell to the ground, covering their heads with their arms.

Then a big white mother duck appeared with three babies in tow.

"Ooohh, did we startle you?" she asked.

Euripides, Rip, and Jesse got up and brushed themselves off.

"Ahh," Rip stuttered. "We just expected something else." Rip gave Abbey a look that said we didn't know you really meant a "duck."

Abbey covered her mouth with her paw and giggled at the joke.

Looking at their clothes, the mother duck questioned, "Are you going to a costume ball?"

Excitedly, Jesse said, "No, we're on a *quesh* for treasure! See our map?"

Rip held up the roll of paper he was carrying and corrected his sister. "*Quest— a quest* for treasure."

"Well, I guess I'm pretty lucky then," sighed the mother duck.

"How so, madam?" questioned Euripides.

"You see, I have my treasure with me—" she gently flapped her wings to indicate her children. "And I didn't need a map to find them."

"You are fortunate, indeed," Euripides said.

"Well, good luck to you on your quack-qua— quest," said the mother, as she led her brood off for a swim.

As the ducks waddled down the path, Rip commented, "Gee, I suppose a treasure can be something different for each of us, huh?"

The friends nodded in agreement as they moved on through the thicket.

Soon they stopped to rest. That's when something buzzed over their heads.

"What was that?" said Abbey.

"Did you see what I saw?" Rip added.

Before anyone could answer, a strange flying creature hovered above them. His long glowing wings never stopped moving– and he wore the strangest oversized goggles!

Euripides smiled. "I should have known. No one knows this thicket better than Sam Aritan, a dragonfly and good friend of mine."

"Can we tell him we're looking for treasure?" asked Jesse, in a loud whisper.

"You just did, little mouse," said Sam, with a grin. Then his face turned serious.

"Hmm? A treasure? In this thicket?" The dragonfly was doubtful as he flew over and studied the map. "Is that 'X' the spot you're trying to find?" he asked, shaking his head.

"That's it," Rip confirmed.

"Ahhh, I know where that is. Not exactly what I'd call treasure though," he stated matter-of-factly. Then as quickly as he had appeared, he disappeared into the thicket.

"What did he mean by that?" questioned Rip, both concerned and mystified.

"Let's find out," Abbey encouraged.

"Onward, me hearties!" Euripides shouted.

Within minutes, they entered a small clearing and their eyes focused on a most magnificent sight.

"Wow!" they all said in awe.

"It's just like the one in the book," said Jesse, holding Bunny so the doll could see, too.

"This is spectacular," added Abbey.

"Amazing," Euripides remarked.

"Gee, Sam sure was wrong!" an overjoyed Rip exclaimed. "This really *is* a treasure!!!"

"How do we get on board?" Rip asked.

"'Tis easy," came a voice from above. Abbey, Rip, and Jesse looked up and saw Euripides on the deck of the ship.

"How did you get up there so fast?" asked Abbey.

"Why, I simply leapt before you looked." Then he added, "Come join me— arghhh, and make it snappy!"

So they did.

"Finding a treasure and capturing a ship all at once— I almost feel like a real pirate," Rip said as he looked around the old vessel.

"Capturing ships and finding treasure is what pirates do best," Jesse commented.

"We're as lucky as the duck!" Abbey added.

Euripides laughed. "We are lucky, indeed. The treasure we found may not be a treasure to everyone, but it's certainly a treasure to us."

"Just think of the adventures we can have now!" Rip said excitedly.

"Yes, and every pirate ship needs one of these," Euripides said as he pulled something black from inside his jacket.

"I have a flag, too." Jesse waved the white and red cloth that was hidden in her pocket.

"A heart!?" shouted Euripides. "I've never seen a pirate flag like that."

Jesse looked rather hurt and a little troubled. "But *our* pirate ship should have one of these, too," Jesse argued. "It shows what kind of pirates we really are."

"We're more than just pirates," Abbey added. "We're a family. A heart says that."

"A heart says we found more than pirate's treasure. We found *true* treasure," said Rip.

Euripides grinned. "You're right. We shall compromise and fly both flags. That way, everyone will know who we're pretending to be and who we really are."

Jesse smiled and hugged Euripides.

With that settled, *Captain* Euripides ordered, "Prepare to set sail, maties!"

They hoisted the sails and jumped up and down on the deck to rock the ship loose. The old vessel creaked and moaned. Suddenly, it was free. . . and the slow current and gentle breeze carried the little ship and her happy crew downstream.

Rip Squeak couldn't wait to find out what new treasure awaited them on their next adventure. Rip just knew that whatever was yet to be discovered, he already had the best treasure of all— his wonderful friends.

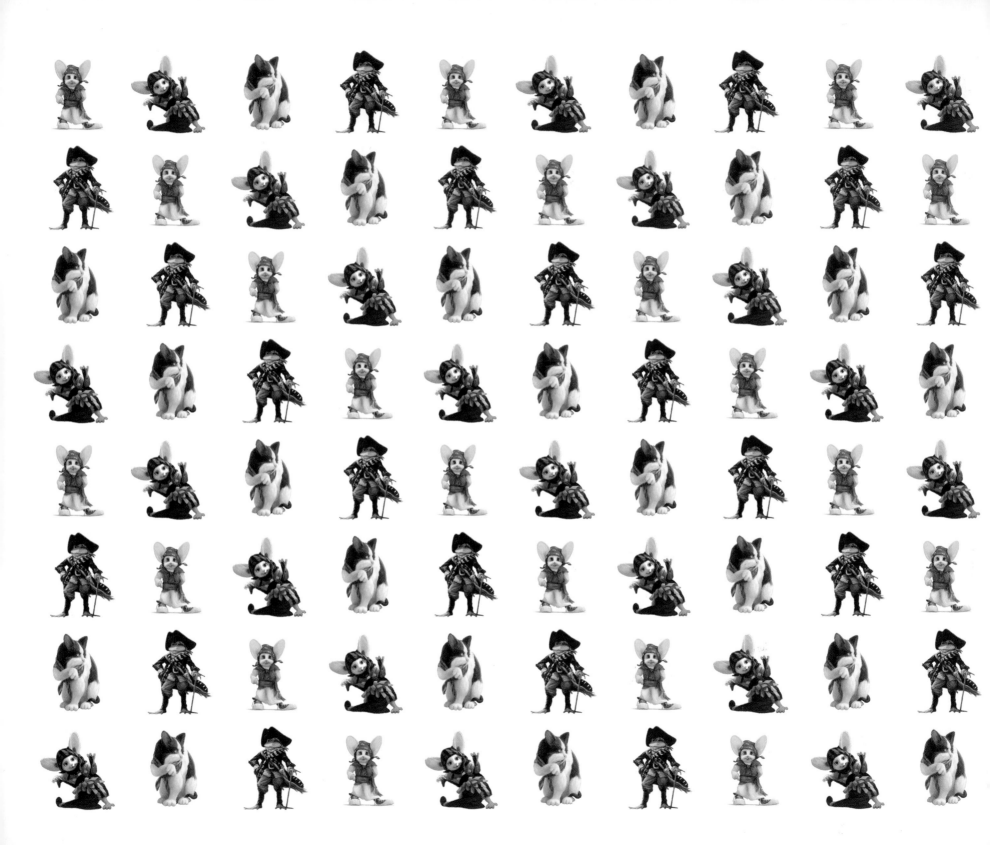